BASEBALL'S BUMBLERS

Baseball is a game of rules and careful moves. From the manager to the last man in the lineup, everyone knows exactly what to do.

But what happens when the sun blinds a fielder chasing a fly ball?

What does a player do when the ball gets lost in his pants?

Where does a base runner run after he's run past a teammate already on base?

What do you call a catcher who throws a potato into the game?

When the unexpected happens in baseball, anything can happen. And it does!

Baseball's Bumblers is a collection of the wacky ways things can go wrong on the diamond.

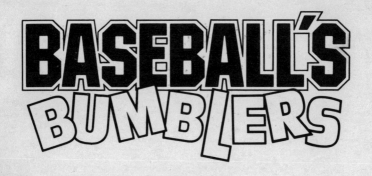

BASEBALL'S BUMBLERS

By D. J. Arneson

Illustrated by Pamiel Barcita

Packaged by Paterson Productions, Inc.

Western Publishing Company, Inc., Racine, Wisconsin 53404

DROPKICKED HOMER

Lou Clinton was a rookie outfielder for the Boston Red Sox in a game between the Sox and the Cleveland Indians. The score was 3-3. Cleveland had a runner on and two outs in the bottom of the fifth. The next Cleveland batter swung hard and connected. The ball soared toward the right field fence.

Clinton raced to catch it. The ball hit the fence and bounced into the air toward the running rookie.

Player and ball arrived at the same place at the same time. The ball hit Clinton's toe. It was a perfect kick. The ball sailed over the fence—for a dropkicked home run because it had not yet touched the ground! To add insult to the red-faced player's bumbler, the home run won the game for the Indians.

BASEBALL'S
BIGGEST BUMBLER

The Abner Doubleday Myth

Everyone *thinks* Abner Doubleday laid out the first baseball diamond in Cooperstown, New York, in 1839, but he didn't.

In 1905, the Spalding Commission was appointed to find out who did. It was named after a sporting goods manufacturer who wanted to prove that baseball was invented in the U.S.A.

The commission received a letter from a man who said his childhood buddy, Abner Doubleday, scratched plans for a new game in the dust of the village green in Cooperstown. Well, there you have it, the commission said, baseball was invented by Abner Doubleday.

But the man was just five years old in 1839 and Doubleday was 20. Also, although Doubleday became a well-known Civil War hero and wrote many articles, he never mentioned baseball!

The truth is, the rules for modern baseball were written by New York Knickerbocker Alexander J. Cartwright in 1845. The Spalding Commission knew this, but chose to ignore it.

Baseball's biggest bumbler is also its oldest!

9

BALK WALK

Bo Jackson, Kansas City Royals, 1986

Bo knows a lot, but once he didn't know the difference between a walk and a balk.

A batter earns a walk—a free trip to first base—when a pitcher tosses four balls. A balk is when a pitcher makes an illegal motion like going into a windup as if to pitch the ball, and then doesn't. The difference is clear. Or is it?

In his first season with the pros, superstar Bo Jackson stepped up to the plate in a game against the California Angels. He cocked his bat, ready to knock the ball out of the park. He swung at the first two pitches and missed. Bo raised his mighty bat to swing again.

Pitcher Don Sutton threw a fastball. The umpire called, "Ball!" The count was two strikes— one strike short of an out—and one ball—three balls short of a walk. Sutton wound up again, but before he threw, the umpire shouted, "Balk!"

Bo thought he said, "Walk," so he tossed his bat aside and trotted toward first base. He would have stayed there if the first base umpire hadn't told him about the bumbler. Now Bo knows balks *and* walks.

FAST FOOD

Gates Brown, Detroit Tigers, 1968

The rule said no eating in the dugout, but for a big man—and big eater—like Detroit's Gates Brown, it was a rule to be broken.

Brown was a pinch hitter in a game against the Cleveland Indians. All he had to do until he was needed was to watch the action—and stay away from the hot dog stand.

By the sixth inning, Gates was hungry. He slipped out of the dugout and returned with two hot dogs dripping with catsup and mustard. As he chomped into the first dog, manager Mayo Smith told him to go to bat. Gates knew he would be fined if he were caught eating, so he jammed the drooling dogs into his jersey.

Gates went to the plate smelling like a hot dog vendor after a busy day. He hit a double, but to make the play, he had to slide into second on his belly—and hot dogs. The minute he stood up, his secret was out—all over his shirt. He was covered with mashed hot dogs, mustard, and catsup.

Gates's bumbled lunch and brightly stained uniform got a laugh from the fans—and a hundred-dollar fine from manager Mayo.

DOUBLE PARKING

Red Faber, Chicago White Sox, 1917

Baseball bases are just big enough for one player to stand on. If there are more than that, something is seriously wrong. Red Faber, the Chicago White Sox pitcher and Hall of Famer, learned that in a bumbler he pulled during the 1917 World Series.

During game two, Faber learned that two objects cannot occupy the same space at the same time. Faber was not a great hitter. When he made it to second on a rare base hit, he forgot there was another Sox player ahead of him. Faber's hit had moved teammate Buck Weaver to third, where Weaver waited for someone to send him home. He didn't expect a crowd.

Convinced that he could be a bigger hero, Faber decided to steal third. He bent his head low and made a beeline for the bag. Just before he arrived, he dropped into a dramatic slide—straight into his astonished teammate.

Faber was quickly tagged out. Fortunately, his silly bumbler didn't affect his pitching or the outcome of the series, which the Sox won handily, four games to two.

15

BOXED FOX

Casey Stengel, Brooklyn Dodgers, 1912

Casey Stengel, in the outfield during an exhibition game, was bored when he spied a large metal box buried in the ground for the water sprinkler system. His eyes lit up. As the crowd watched a back-and-forth duel between pitcher and batter, Casey got into the box and closed the lid just enough to watch the action.

The crack of the bat announced a hit. The ball soared into the air and dropped toward left field, but there was nobody there! The pop fly and easy out was turning into a hit.

Casey pushed the cover, but it was too heavy to open all the way. He was trapped as the ball fell toward him, too far away to catch. His gag was backfiring.

Suddenly, the ball caught on a puff of wind and floated toward the buried box. Casey held the lid open with one arm and stuck out his gloved hand. The ball landed with a smack for the out! Casey's nearly bumbled joke turned into one of baseball's great stories.

ERROR CIRCUS

New York Mets, 1963

It was a 1-0 ball game between the Mets, who were leading, and the Pittsburgh Pirates in the bottom of the ninth. The Pirates were up, with one man out. Pirate Dick Schofield was on first as the result of a walk when Manny Mota dinked a grounder toward Mets pitcher Galen Cisco. Cisco grabbed for the ball, but it sneaked by.

Second baseman Ron Hunt and shortstop Al Moran took off after the ball, but both missed.

The ball rumbled toward Duke Carmel, the Mets center fielder, but popped into the air and Carmel missed it. Joe Christopher, the right fielder, cornered the elusive ball and tossed a wild throw toward home as Cisco got back into the act. He tripped and fell on his face.

Meanwhile, Pirates Schofield and Mota raced for home. Schofield made it, but Cisco finally fired the ball to catcher Jesse Gonder to stop Mota's winning run. Gonder grabbed the throw and spun around to tag Mota. Mota was already across the plate and Gonder was so far from the plate, it was pointless to try. Mota scored the winning run and the Mets made not one but *six* bumblers on one incredible play!

BUM RUN

Gene Freese, Pittsburgh Pirates, 1955

The last-place Pirates were 31 games out of first place in a 10-inning 4-4 game against the Philadelphia Phillies. The Pirates had two runners on and two outs. Tom Saffell was on third and in scoring position. Gene Freese was on first. A single run would win the game for the Pirates and end their 10-game losing streak.

Ramon Mejias drove a single into center field. Saffell left third and raced home for the winning score. Well, not quite.

Freese knew immediately that Saffell would score on Mejias's hit. He was so excited that instead of running to second and touching the base as he should have, he ran to congratulate Ramon on first for driving in the winning run.

Phillie Richie Ashburn had the ball and knew the rules. He tossed the ball to shortstop Roy Smalley, who put his foot on second base. That meant Freese was forced out.

The umpires ruled the inning ended with the force-out. When play resumed, the Phillies scored four runs to win the game 8-4. Freese's bumbler dropped his team to 32 games out of first and stretched its losing streak to 11!

DUD SPUD

Dave Bresnahan, Williamsport, Pa., 1987

Throwing a dud can happen to any ballplayer, but Dave Bresnahan was tossed out of a game for throwing a spud! Because his minor league career was not going anywhere, Dave came up with a scheme to get some attention.

Dave carved a potato into a baseball and hid the spud in an extra catcher's mitt he kept in the Williamsport team's dugout.

During a game against the team from Reading, Pennsylvania, when Reading had two outs and a runner on third, Dave put his plan into action. He signaled for a time-out and told the ump he wanted to get another mitt from the dugout. He returned behind the plate with the mitt with the potato ball. He held the spud in his right hand, while he took a slow pitch in his mitt. He tossed the potato in a deliberately wild throw over the third baseman's head and the runner on third raced for home. When he arrived, Dave tagged him with the real ball.

The umpire was puzzled, but when he realized Dave had pulled a trick, he threw the catcher out of the game. Dave's joke bumbled because not much later, the team let him go.

YOU'RE OUT—AGAIN!

Andy Van Slyke of the St. Louis Cardinals stepped up to the plate. All eyes in the stadium were on him. The Cards outfielder took a strike, and then another. After the second strike, Andy turned away from the plate and headed for the dugout with the dejected look of a player who had struck out. But he hadn't. He had bumbled the count and still had one strike left.

Fans heckled Andy all the way back to the box. Andy raised his bat. The pitcher wound up. The ball burned toward the plate. "Steeeerike three!" the ump screamed. When Andy slinked back to the dugout this time, he was *really* dejected.

HAT HIT

Larry Biittner, Chicago Cubs, 1979

Larry Biittner, the Chicago Cubs right fielder, heard the crack of the bat when Bruce Boisclair of the New York Mets slugged a long ball toward him. The Cub made a mad dash for the ball but couldn't get under it. His hat flew off as he made a last-effort dive. When he got to his feet, Larry stared into his glove, but the ball wasn't there. Meanwhile, Boisclair was burning toward first.

Biittner frantically searched for the missing ball as Boisclair continued his thundering race around the bases. The ball was not in the grass or in the area between the edge of the outfield and the fence. It was gone for good.

Totally frustrated, Biittner watched helplessly as Boisclair started toward third. Larry bent down to get his cap and—surprise!—there was the ball. He managed to fire a streaking throw to his third baseman, who tagged Boisclair, but by this time the stadium was quaking with laughter. Luckily, Larry Biittner's bumbler didn't cost him more than a red face.

BALL-BOTTOMED TROUSERS

Dutch Leonard, Washington Senators, 1945

Dutch Leonard was a pitcher back in the days of baggy baseball pants that were known more for room than good looks.

Leonard fired a pitch to Philadelphia Athletics Irvin Hall and Hall walloped it straight back into Leonard's stomach, bending him over double. Stung but not dead, Leonard slapped his glove over his stomach to trap the ball, but when he reached for the ball to throw it to first, his glove was empty.

Suspecting he had dropped the ball, Leonard scoured the ground with eagle eyes, but the ball wasn't there, either. He looked all over the mound and infield and came up empty.

Leonard's stomach hadn't stopped vibrating from the hit when he felt another odd sensation. This one was in his leg. It was the ball. It had found an opening and had scurried down the pitcher's baggy pants like a gopher down its hole.

With a red face, Leonard dug the ball out of his pants, but by then it was too late. Hall, the batter, was safely on first, thanks to Leonard's bumbler with his ball-bottom pants.

FANATIC FAN

Babe Ruth, New York Yankees, 1927

Baseball's immortal Babe Ruth was in his record-setting 60-homer season and was as eager as his fans for another home run. One fan, a young boy, was especially eager.

In a game against the Detroit Tigers, the youngster screamed for a hit each time Ruth stepped to the plate.

The Babe heard him. On his fourth at bat, the home run king blasted the ball into the right field bleachers and set off on his familiar trot around the bases with his bat on his shoulder.

The kid wanted more. He jumped onto the diamond and caught up with his hero as he rounded third. He grabbed Babe's bat and pulled, but baseball's most famous player held tight. The two played a game of tug-of-war for the bat as they both ran toward home. Since the kid wouldn't let go, the Babe simply dragged him over the plate and then to the Yankee dugout.

The plucky kid's bumbled grab for the Babe's mighty bat made the papers, and for a day, he, too, was a baseball hero.

STALL BALL

Paul LaPalme, Chicago White Sox, 1957

How hard can it be for a pitcher to simply stand on the mound and hold the ball? Very hard, it seems, for a pitcher named Paul LaPalme.

LaPalme was sent into a game against the Baltimore Orioles to finish up a winning game by stalling for time. The White Sox were ahead, 4-3. Because the Chicago team had to catch a train after the game, both teams and officials agreed to end the game at precisely 10:20.

The game went to nine innings. With two minutes left, LaPalme was sent in to stall for time and a Sox win.

Rather than count moths fluttering around the lights, LaPalme pitched. He threw a strike and a ball. He threw another pitch just seconds before 10:20.

The ball headed straight for the strike zone. The batter laid into the ball and sent it on a one-way flight into the bleachers for a home run that tied the game, 4-4, just as the clock ticked 10:20.

Instead of winning the game, LaPalme's bumbler lost it because the tie game had to be replayed later and the Orioles won!

FIELDING FOLLIES

St. Louis Browns, 1944

The St. Louis Browns, in the field in a World Series game against the St. Louis Cardinals, expected a bunt from Cards batter Max Lanier. The Cards had a man on first. A sacrifice bunt would advance him to scoring position.

The batter popped a short bunt toward third. Red Hayworth, the Browns catcher, Mark Christman, the third baseman, and Nelson Potter, the pitcher, dashed for it. Suddenly they all stopped, each thinking the other had it. The ball lay on the grass as the batter burned toward first. The pitcher grabbed the ball, but dropped it. He finally got it under control, but tossed wild over the second baseman, who was covering first.

Outfielder Gene Moore raced after the elusive ball as the runner sped around the bases. Moore bent over, but the ball shot through his legs. He picked up the ball—and dropped it! Completely bent out of shape by the series of bumblers, Moore grabbed the ball and hurled it toward second. The ball flew over the second baseman's head for an incredible total of eight bumblers on one play! To make matters worse, the runner made it to third and Lanier was safe on first!

YOU'RE SAFE,
BUT YOU'RE OUT!

Granny Hamner of the Philadelphia Phillies didn't know when to keep his mouth shut. Hamner had just popped a short hit that was fielded by Johnny Logan and quickly tossed to Frank Torre, playing first base. Hamner poured on the steam to beat the ball, but it would be close.

Luckily, Logan's toss was wide and Torre had to take his foot off the bag. He snagged the ball and then spun, hoping to tag Hamner, who flew in at full speed. Torre missed.

Relieved, Hamner shouted, "No!" as he slipped by Torre's glove.

The ump did not like the idea of someone else making his calls and Hamner felt like arguing. In seconds the two were hammering it out verbally. "Say one more word and you're out," the ump said.

"One more word," Hamner said with a grin.

The ump meant what he said and threw Hamner—who was safe—out.

BUMBLING BALL

George Cutshaw, Brooklyn Dodgers, 1913

How can a grounder turn into a home run?
When it jumps over the outfield fence.

It was a tight game between the Brooklyn Dodgers and the Philadelphia Phillies at Ebbets Field. George Cutshaw, a notorious home run hitter, was at bat in the bottom of the eleventh inning of the tied ball game. At the pitch, Cutshaw swung hard, but managed to only hit the ball down the first base line. He took off for first.

The ball sped into the outfield as the Phillies right fielder chased it. Cutshaw headed for second. The ball sizzled over the grass and shot up an embankment in front of the outfield fence. The outfielder was certain the ball would ricochet off the fence to his poised glove. But it didn't. Still steaming, it whizzed up the bank and over the fence—out of the park!

Cutshaw circled the bases and tagged home to score on the only ground ball homer in baseball history.

2 + 1 = 4?

Ron Cey, Steve Garvey,
Los Angeles Dodgers, 1980

Sometimes it takes two to bumble. Ron Cey and Steve Garvey of the L.A. Dodgers tried it in a game against the New York Mets, and it worked.

Cey was up. Garvey was on second. Cey raised his bat. The count was two and two. The pitch blew by and the ump called, "Ball three!" Cey flipped his bat aside and started down the first base line, believing he had earned a walk.

When Garvey saw Cey trotting toward first, he figured his own count was off and Cey was right, so he took off for third. A glance at the scoreboard cleared up the arithmetic error instantly. Garvey was caught between second and third. He raced back toward second.

Mets catcher John Stearns, a math whiz who could add 2 +1 and get 3, pegged the ball to his second baseman, who tagged Garvey as the red-faced runner desperately tried to get back to safety. In the meantime, Cey, who started the two-man bumbler with his lousy addition, returned to the plate to finish his time at bat.

KNOCK-KNOCK

Baltimore Orioles, 1894

Baseball teams have players, managers, coaches, trainers, owners, and fans. One even had a doorkeeper.

The Baltimore Orioles were in a 3-3 game with the New York Giants in the bottom of the ninth inning when an Orioles batter hit toward the Giants shortstop. The shortstop tossed a wild throw toward first that flew over the first baseman's head, bounced, and then rolled toward the clubhouse door. Sitting next to the door was Tommy Murphy, the Orioles groundskeeper.

When Tommy saw the ball speeding toward the closed door, he saw his chance to help his team. He leaped from his chair, ran to the door, and jerked it open just as the ball arrived. It rolled through the open door. Tommy jumped in after the ball and locked the door behind him as the Orioles runner rounded the bases toward home and the winning run.

Once he knew his team had scored, Tommy opened the door with a smile. It was baseball's first win by a "door prize."

BATTY BATTER

José Nunez, Toronto Blue Jays, 1988

The first time José Nunez went to bat in his pro career was a laughter disaster. As a pitcher in the American League, José's turns at bat were taken by designated hitters, so he never had to face a fastball. But at spring training one year, José's Blue Jays were playing the Philadelphia Phillies, a National League team. The National League did not permit designated hitters. That meant José would have to step up to the plate.

José acted like a batter. He spit into the dirt and waved his bat like a two-handed sword. The umpire tapped him on the shoulder and suggested José take off his warm-up jacket.

Unembarrassed, left-handed José waggled his bat again. The umpire reminded him to put on a left-handed batting helmet. José just put his right-handed hat on backward. The umpire told him to put on the correct hat. Rather than go to the dugout for another helmet, José stepped to the other side of the plate to bat right-handed.

José's bumbling in the batter's box didn't produce any hits, but it did fill the stands with laughter.

HOME PLATE HOP

Hank Gowdy, New York Giants, 1924

Hank Gowdy was the New York Giants catcher in the final game of the 1924 World Series between the Giants and the Washington Senators. The game had gone 12 innings and the score was tied, 3-3. Washington was at bat. A run would win the game and the series.

Gowdy was behind the plate and Muddy Ruel was at bat. At the pitch, Muddy swung and connected, but the ball went straight up. Gowdy stepped back, tossed his mask to the ground, and raised his mitt to catch the pop-up for an easy out. His foot landed in his upturned mask as neatly as if he'd put it into a wastepaper basket.

The ball plunged to the ground. Gowdy tried to get under it, but the mask was like a brake and all he could do was hop. He danced faster and faster, shaking his leg as if trying to kick off a clod of mud. The ball plopped safely to the ground, ending Gowdy's chance for an easy out.

The mask-foot bumbler gave Ruel another crack at the ball that got him a two-base hit. A teammate's single drove Ruell home and the Senators won the series!

TWO-BASE HOME RUN

Josh Gibson, a well-known catcher in the old Negro National League, was a powerful hitter. Unfortunately, by the time he reached his late forties, he wasn't much of a runner.

In a game at Dexter Park between the Grays and the Bushwicks, Gibson, a Gray, walloped a 500-foot drive straight through center field. There were no fences at Dexter Park, so the ball just kept on going.

Gibson took off from home plate the moment he hit the ball. He huffed and puffed his way to first before anyone realized how far the ball had traveled. A fast runner would have rounded second, eaten up third, and trotted home on the incredible home run hit, but Gibson was anything but fast.

Too bushed to run farther than second base, Gibson sat down on the bag and turned his 500-footer into a bumbled double.

BASES UNLOADED

Ricky Peters, Oakland Athletics, 1986

It was the top of the ninth in a game between the Oakland A's and the Kansas City Royals. The score was tied, 4-4. A single run could win the game if everything else went well. Things went well for the Royals, but not for the A's because somebody bumbled.

With a half inning to go, Jerry Willard of the A's singled to first. Ricky Peters went in to run for him as a pinch runner. A sacrifice out moved him to second. The next batter earned a walk, so now there were two runners on base. Peters was on second and Carney Lansford was on first. The Royals pitcher threw wild and both A's moved up one base. Peters was now in scoring position on third.

Jose Canseco was at bat for the A's. He drew four balls and earned a walk. As he headed for first, Peters started toward home because he thought the bases were loaded!

It was too late for him to get back to safety when he realized his bumbler. He made a sliding try, but was tagged out. The A's didn't get their run, but the Royals scored in the bottom of the ninth and won the game!

TRIPLE DIPPER

Brooklyn Dodgers, 1926

This bumbler drove in a winning run on a two-base hit that ended with two outs at third!

Floyd Herman was at bat for the Brooklyn Dodgers in a 1-1 ball game against the Boston Braves. The bases were loaded. Chick Fewster was on first, Dazzy Vance on second, and Hank DeBerry on third.

Herman blasted a line drive into right field. DeBerry ran home to score. Vance and Fewster advanced as Herman slid into second. Herman saw a Dodger trapped between home and third in a rundown. He thought it was Fewster, the man ahead of him, and headed for third. But there already was a Dodger on third—Fewster. The Dodger caught in the rundown was Vance.

Suddenly Vance broke away from the Braves trying to tag him and headed back to third. He slid into the crowd of Dodgers already there. The Braves third baseman couldn't believe his eyes. He tagged the bumbling Dodgers as fast as he could. Vance was safe, but Fewster and Herman were out. Luckily, DeBerry's run won the game.

HUMBLING BUMBLERS

Jackie Mitchell, Chattanooga, 1931

The owner of the Chattanooga Lookouts hired Jackie Mitchell, a 17-year-old girl, to pitch against the New York Yankees in an exhibition game as a publicity stunt.

Jackie was a great pitcher, but in her first trip to the mound she had to face three of baseball's most famous hitters, Babe Ruth, Lou Gehrig, and Tony Lazzeri.

The Babe was first to bumble. He swung at two of Jackie's sinkers and then took a ball. Jackie burned a fastball past the Sultan of Swat for a called strike—and the mighty Ruth was out!

Then Lou Gehrig stepped up. Jackie whipped three straight sinkers over the plate and Gehrig struck at—and missed—every one!

Lazzeri was lucky. He drew four balls and walked, but the Yankees dugout was red with embarrassment. Jackie left the game to the approving roar of the crowd, the first woman to officially play in a professional baseball game.

BUM THROW

Dave Winfield, San Diego Padres, 1974

Nobody could accuse Dave Winfield of not following instructions in a game between the San Diego Padres and the Montreal Expos.

The Padres outfielders were having trouble relaying the ball to the infield. The object is to toss to a teammate—the cutoff man—in the center of the diamond, who can then throw the ball to where it will do the most good.

Winfield's tosses were going wild, so manager John McNamara told him over and over to hit the cutoff man.

Montreal had a man on second when an Expo batter hit a single toward Dave. The ball had to be relayed home to stop a possible run.

Winfield snapped up the ball and fired a streaking throw toward home.

The Padres second baseman, Derrel Thomas, knew Winfield could make the throw to the plate, so he would not be needed as cutoff man. Thomas bent over double to let the ball sizzle by. The ball sizzled, but not by Thomas's ear. Winfield, perhaps still hearing manager McNamara's pleas to "hit the cutoff man," burned a stinger smack into Thomas's target-sized backside!

BUMBLING UMP

Emmett Ashford, 1968

Umpires are supposed to be neutral, but sometimes their timing is off, as Emmett Ashford, the second base ump in a game between the Baltimore Orioles and the New York Yankees, learned.

The Orioles were leading, 5-3, in the bottom of the eighth. An error got Yank Joe Pepitone to first, where he waited to be advanced or to steal if he got the chance.

Boog Powell, the Orioles first baseman, decided to fake Pepitone off the base and then tag him with a hidden ball. He strolled to the pitcher's mound with the ball, but did not call time-out as he should have. He faked handing off the ball to the Orioles pitcher, but kept it in his glove. Boog would tag Pepitone when he returned to first.

Umpire Ashford realized Boog had not called time-out. So, good ump that he was, Ashford boomed a loud "Time out!" that echoed through the stands.

Boog's shoulders slumped. The ump correctly but mistakenly bumbled the first baseman's plot, and Joe Pepitone remained safely on first.

THREE BUMBLERS IN ONE

Tommy John, New York Yankees, 1988

New York Yankees pitcher Tommy John learned that some records should be left alone.

In 1898, New York Giants pitcher J. Bentley Seymour committed three errors in one inning. In 1988, Tommy John did better than that.

The Yankees were leading the Milwaukee Brewers, 4-0, in the fourth inning when a batter hit a dribbler toward the pitcher's mound. John grabbed the ball but dropped it for an error. The runner on first dashed to second while the batter headed to first.

John picked up the ball and winged a wild throw toward first. The ball sailed into right field for John's second error.

The runner on second raced toward home as runner number two headed for second. The right fielder grabbed John's overthrow and tossed it at the Yankee catcher to stop the runner coming from third.

Rather than let the ball go by, John intercepted it and threw another wild throw for his third error. He not only tied Seymour's record, he managed to make all three errors in one play! To add insult to injury, both runners scored.

ATTENTION, PLEASE!

Cleveland Indians, 1983

A slow baseball game can be boring, but once a whole baseball team wasn't paying attention.

It was the bottom of the sixth in a game between the last-place Cleveland Indians and the wide-awake Kansas City Royals. The Royals were at bat. Neal Heaton was pitching for the Indians.

The first Royal to bat, Hal McRae, took four balls and walked. That put one man on with no outs. The next batter, Amos Otis, connected for a grounder. An Indian fielder snagged the ball and whipped it to first. Otis was tagged for out number one. The first baseman pegged the ball to second. It arrived an instant before McRae did and he was tagged out. The double play knocked off two Royals for two outs. Another would retire the side.

But one side was already prepared to retire. The moment the double play ended, pitcher Heaton headed for the dugout as if he'd just knocked off three, not two, Royals. And the rest of the Indians followed, just like the sheep they must have been counting. Last place goes to those who earn it.

ILLEGAL PASSING

Dan Ford, Minnesota Twins, 1978

The Minnesota Twins were losing, 4-0, in the bottom of the seventh against the Chicago White Sox when three Twins got on base. Dan Ford was on third, José Morales was on second, and Larry Wolfe was on first. All three were ready to roll when Bombo Rivera hit a single into center field.

Dan Ford started toward home, but in his excitement decided to encourage Morales, right behind him, to turn on the steam. Ford ran backward, hollering at José to head for home.

José left second, rounded third, and headed toward the plate. Ford got so caught up in his coaching role that he stopped before he reached the bag. José shot by him and scored. Suddenly, Ford realized his incredible bumbler. By letting José pass, Ford doomed him to an out because passing is illegal. José's score was no good.

Dan quickly slapped his foot onto home plate, but the White Sox catcher had seen the whole thing. He complained to the umpire and José was called out.

Dan Ford's bumbler cost his team a run and the game because Chicago beat Minnesota, 4-3.

NO
PASSING
ZONE

THE OLDEST TRICK IN BASEBALL

Jimmy Piersall, Boston Red Sox, 1953

Every kid has tried the old "hidden ball" trick once. That's as often as it works because after you've seen it, you'll never be fooled again. But even the pros forget.

In a game with the St. Louis Browns, Boston's Jimmy Piersall was on second. A pop fly was caught and the ball tossed to the Browns shortstop, Billy Hunter, who took it to the mound.

Instead of giving the pitcher the ball, Hunter hid it in his glove and returned to his position. He glanced at the bag. "That bag's covered with dirt," he told the unsuspecting runner. "Give it a kick to knock the dirt off."

"Sure," Piersall said. He stepped off the bag and was instantly tagged by Hunter, who slapped the hidden ball against him as if he were swatting a mosquito.

"You're out!" the umpire shouted.

Old tricks never die...because they still work.

KLEM'S DILEMMA

Bill Klem, 1913

An ump's big bumble cost a team its winning run. The ump was Bill Klem, a National League umpire known for his stubbornness.

The New York Giants and the Philadelphia Phillies were in a tenth-inning scoreless tie when New York quickly filled the bases. The team smelled victory when Moose McCormick came in to pinch hit for pitcher Al Demaree. Umpire Klem turned to the stadium and in his loudest voice explained the change in the lineup while the game continued behind his back.

Moose knocked a fastball into left field and raced for first. The Giants on base advanced, and Fred Merkle scored from third to win the game.

The stands erupted with excitement as the teams headed for the showers. Moose McCormick was elated that he drove in the winning run.

But it was not to be. Umpire Klem ruled that the ball was out of play while he was making his lineup change announcement to the crowd. He said the run didn't count and the game had to be resumed. When it finally ended due to darkness, the score was still 0-0, thanks to the ump's bumbler.

PASS IT ON

Chicago Cubs, 1966

Teamwork wins games, but once it almost stole one for the Chicago Cubs in a game with the San Francisco Giants.

A Giant hit the ball deep into center field. The Cub rookie center fielder, Byron Browne, ran for it at full speed. He hit the fence and fell to the ground as the ball bounced 20 feet away.

Browne reached into the grass a couple of feet away and threw a ball to a Cubs infielder, who relayed the toss to third. The batter was out.

The Giants suspected trickery. The batted ball had bounded 20 feet from Browne. The one he threw was within reach. Players, managers, and umpires converged on the fallen Cub. A teammate found the lost game ball and hid it in his shirt. A Giant saw the move, so the Cub gave the ball to another teammate, who passed it on.

The ball Browne had tossed for the out was retrieved. It was a beat-up batting practice ball that had been forgotten in the grass.

The umpire made the Cubs and their trainer line up. The real ball was handed over and the bumbled teamwork trick was discovered.

SLIDE, WILLIE, SLIDE!

Willie Stargell, Pittsburgh Pirates, 1978

Willie Stargell played first base for the Pittsburgh Pirates, but this time he was on first as the result of a hit. He glanced at Pittsburgh manager Chuck Tanner in the dugout. Willie blinked. Tanner signaled Willie to steal second base!

For another runner, a steal sign made sense, but Willie was not a runner. At 38 years old, he wasn't exactly in his prime. A bit of extra weight around the middle didn't help. But the manager was boss, so Willie made a beeline—or rather, a bumblebeeline—for second.

It was hopeless. When Willie was barely over halfway to the bag, it was clear he wouldn't make it. Since he couldn't get back to first, he decided to slide for second. That made as much sense as thinking a bowling ball could coast uphill.

Willie hit the ground and rumbled to a stop 10 feet from the bag. The Cubs shortstop closed in to tag him out. Willie leaped to his feet, made a "T" sign, and called, "Time out!"

It was Willie who was out, of course, but his bumbled steal and illegal time-out call won a round of laughter from the fans.

UMP'S BOO-BOO

Umpire Bill Klem took pride in his calls and claimed that he was never wrong. That's arguable, because at one game in 1913, the always-right ump was definitely wrong.

Klem was being heckled by the players in the Pirates dugout. He decided he wasn't going to take any more. He walked up to the players and said he would toss the next player who talked back to him out of the game.

When the next Pirate player stepped up to the plate, Klem asked him for his name. The young player mumbled something that Klem could not hear. He hollered at the kid to speak up.

The player, a rookie, turned around to the ump and said, "Booe!"

Klem turned red. "That's it," he shouted. "I warned you. You're out of the game."

The Pirates manager raced to the plate. "You called it wrong this time," he told the angry ump.

Klem fumed. "I asked the kid his name and he said, 'Boo!' Nobody gets away with that."

"This one does," the manager said. "His name is Booe. Everitt Booe."

BUMPING BUMBLERS

Tom McCraw, Washington Senators, 1971

An inside-the-park homer is rare because there are usually enough players to cover any situation. But if three fielders meet unexpectedly, anything can happen.

Tom McCraw of the Washington Senators was at bat against the Cleveland Indians. He hit a blooper fly into left center field, an easy out. Three Indian fielders moved in for the catch.

Shortstop Jack Heidman ran backward as the ball sailed over his head. He called for the ball. So did Vada Pinson, the center fielder. John Lowenstein hustled for the blooped fly from left field. None of the players saw the others and they all collided with a thud. They fell as the ball dribbled to a stop nearby.

Batter McCraw raced to first, ran to second, and poured on the steam for third as Indian second baseman Eddie Leon retrieved the ball. McCraw headed for home. Leon winged a sizzler to his catcher, but McCraw slid under the ball and was safe—an inside-the-park homer!

The three bumbling fielders' injuries were treated, but nothing could be done for their hurt pride.

VANISHING BALL

Eddie Joost, Philadelphia Athletics, 1948

In a game against the Boston Red Sox, Eddie Joost, the Philadelphia Athletics shortstop, almost gave the shirt off his back to field a bumbled ball.

Joost was in the field when a short infield hit sneaked past Bill McCahan, the A's pitcher. Backing up the play, Joost ran for the ball, grabbed for it, and straightened up to throw to first. The trouble was, he didn't have the ball.

Joost glanced at the grass around his feet, but the ball was gone. In the meantime, the Sox hitter reached first while a second Sox runner scooted to third. Suddenly the truth hit Joost. The ball had shot up the inside of his sleeve and was now stuck inside the back of his jersey.

Everyone on the field and in the stadium began to chuckle as Joost tried to reach around his back to get the ball, but couldn't quite reach it. He danced a jig to shake it loose, but that didn't work, either. As a last resort, Joost started to unbutton his shirt, but even that took too much time, so he pulled the shirt out of his pants. The ball fell out amid roars of laughter, including Joost's own at his unexpected bumbler.

THREE-BASE STRIKEOUT

Paul Ratliff, Minnesota Twins, 1970

Minnesota Twins catcher Paul Ratliff was behind the plate as Detroit Tiger Earl Wilson stepped up to bat. Wilson took two strikes and missed a third, but Ratliff dropped it.

When a catcher drops a third strike, he has to either tag the batter or toss the ball to first base to make the out. But Ratliff lazily tossed the ball toward the pitcher's mound and headed for the dugout. The other Twins did the same.

The Tigers third base coach realized the error. He waited until most of the Twins were off the field and then told Wilson to run to first base. Wilson, unnoticed, chugged to first, ran past second, and headed for third.

A straggling Twins fielder saw what was happening. He grabbed the ball and called to his teammates as Wilson raced toward home. A quick toss from the fielder stopped him and Wilson tried to make it back to third. The ball caught up with him when a Twin fired it back to the fielder, who now covered third. Wilson was out, but he almost had a home run on Ratliff's bumbler.

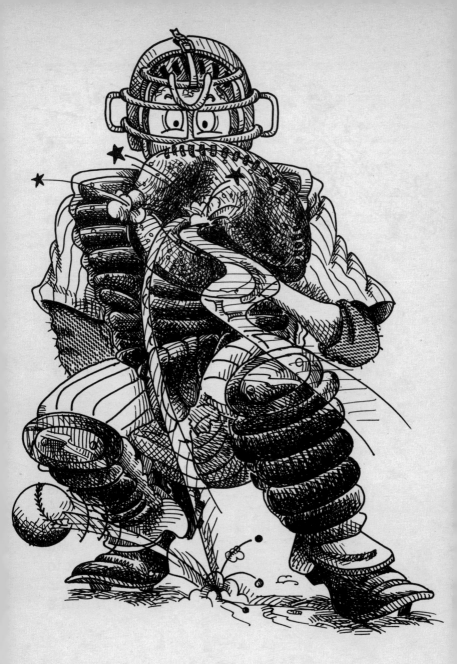

STAR-SPANGLED BUMBLE

Lonny Frey, Cincinnati Reds, 1942

The traditional start of a baseball game is the playing of the national anthem. It's not supposed to favor either team, but once it did, sort of.

The Detroit Tigers and Cincinnati Reds were playing a spring training game. The teams lined up for "The Star-Spangled Banner," but nothing happened because the public address system was broken. The game was started anyway.

The first to bat was Tiger Jimmy Bloodworth. He whacked a grounder to Lonny Frey, the Reds second baseman. It would be an easy snag that Frey could toss to first base for a sure out.

Suddenly the public address speakers filled the air with the National Anthem. The United States had just entered the Second World War less than five months earlier, on December 7, 1941, so the song meant much more than usual.

Frey, already bent over to field the speeding grounder, stood up at the sound. He took off his cap and snapped to rigid attention as the ball skimmed by his feet on the way to the outfield. The second baseman's patriotic bumbler cost his team an easy out.

THE GLUE BLEW

Graig Nettles, New York Yankees, 1974

You don't have to be an engineer to play baseball, but it helps. For example, if a bat is heavier at the end than in the middle, the weight on the end will produce a longer hit. Baseball rules prevent doctoring bats, but rules, like glue, sometimes come unstuck.

Graig Nettles had one home run in a game against the Detroit Tigers and was ready for another. He hefted his bat over his shoulder and with a solid punch, knocked the ball into left field.

Everyone except Tiger catcher Bill Freehan watched the ball. He noticed that when the ball left Nettle's bat, so did a piece of the bat. He picked it up and showed it to the umpire.

The bat wasn't broken. It had been engineered to make the tip heavier than the middle. It's an old trick. The end of the bat is sawed off and a deep hole is bored down the bat's length. The hole is filled with cork and the end is glued back on.

The ump said the bat was illegal, the hit void, and the batter out. Nettle's said a fan gave him the bat. But the fans knew it was untrue and said boo to the bumbler whose glue blew.

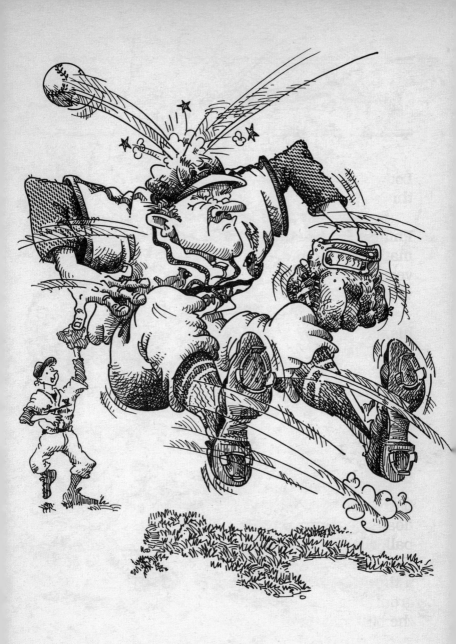

"I GOT IT—OUCH!"

Stan Musial was already a star with the St. Louis Cardinals, but at age 24, he still had a few things to learn.

Stan was in a game against the Philadelphia Phillies in the spring of 1944. One of his teammates was the legendary Pepper Martin, a 40-year-old star himself. Stan played center field while Pepper covered right field.

Musial didn't get many opportunities to show his stuff for most of the game because no balls came his way. He had to be content to wait out the game like everyone else.

Then, in the eighth inning, things began to heat up and the Phillies were starting to smoke. Nobody had time to relax. Stan pumped himself up to be ready for anything, just in case something came his way.

The Phillies put two runners on. The next batter knocked a high fly into center field. Musial floated backward, never taking his eye off the ball. His glove was out—and so was the sun. For a second the ball vanished, only to reappear with a thud right on top of Stan's head. He fell to the ground as Pepper Martin, the old pro, picked up the ball and made the play!

TRICK CATCH

Rennie Stennett,
Pittsburgh Pirates, 1976

Sometimes, baseball is boring. Suddenly, the crack of the bat signals a hit and all eyes follow the play. A trick would be impossible. *Wrong.*

The Los Angeles Dodgers were at bat. Rennie Stennett was covering second for the Pirates, Willie Stargell was at first, and Dave Parker was in right field. A short fly popped into right field. Parker, a 230-pounder, and Stargell, 210 pounds, raced for the ball. Stennett, who weighed a mere 160 pounds, ran to make the catch.

The two heavyweights closed in on the ball with Stennett caught between them. Rather than get smashed like a bug, Stennett stepped out of the way. The two big players crashed into one another and fell to the ground. So did the ball, but nobody noticed.

As the two dazed players shook the cobwebs from their heads, Stennett picked up the ball and put it in Willie Stargell's glove. He whispered to Willie to stand and show the ball to the umpire. When Stargell waved the ball, the umpire turned to the batter and shouted, "Out!"

It was a trick catch that nobody caught.

HOMER BONER

Tim McCarver,
Philadelphia Phillies, 1976

A batter's greatest triumph is a home run with the bases loaded. A grand slam homer is rare, but that's what makes it exciting. Add a mixup to a grand slam and you get a Class A bumbler.

The Philadelphia Phillies were playing the Pittsburgh Pirates. Tim McCarver of the Phillies was at bat with the bases loaded. He connected with a pitch that sent the ball over the back fence for a batter's dream, a grand slammer. McCarver tucked his head into his chest and began his home run trot around the bases.

He should have kept his head up. The Philly already on first, Garry Maddox, did. He saw McCarver's hit leave the park, but just before it was safely gone, he returned to first in case a Pirate outfielder snagged it. Meanwhile, McCarver was burning toward first.

McCarver, thrilled with his homer, raced past Maddox. Suddenly the truth hit him. A runner who passes another runner is automatically out. And he was. McCarver's bumbler cost him a perfect grand slammer.

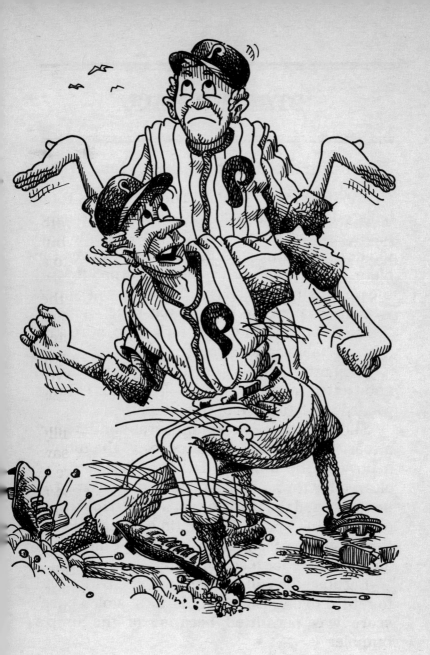

STALLED CALL

Fred Clarke, Pittsburgh Pirates, 1906

The bases were loaded. The count was three balls, one strike. Fred Clarke, Pittsburgh's player-manager, was on third, ready to dash home. The pitcher wound up and laid a streaker over the plate. Every head in the stadium turned toward the umpire to hear the call. The ump was silent.

Clarke knew the ump would have shouted, "Strike!" if the pitch were a strike. So, sure that it was a ball, Clarke strolled home.

The batter also assumed the pitch was a ball and trotted to first on a walk. The Cubs catcher winged the ball back to the pitcher.

Suddenly the silent stadium was shattered by a roar. *"Steeeeerikkkkke twoooooo!"* the umpire bellowed. The umpire's face was beet red. He cleared his throat and explained that just as the pitch crossed the plate, he got a frog in his throat and couldn't speak. By the time he cleared his throat, the batter was on first and Clarke had ambled home for a score.

Because the call was a strike, the batter had to return to bat. But Fred Clarke's "stolen base" score was permitted because of the ump's bumbler.

UNBROKEN RECORDS

Harley Parker, Cincinnati Reds, 1901

Records are made to be broken, but two records by one bumbler should be forgotten.

Harley "Doc" Parker was an enthusiastic player, but a lousy pitcher. The Cincinnati Reds were looking for help out of the basement and signed Doc as a pitcher.

Doc took the mound against the World Series-winning Brooklyn Dodgers. It looked like David versus Goliath.

Almost every Dodger got a hit. They grew so tired of hitting and running that by the eighth inning they stopped trying. They knocked wimpy hits that were gathered by exhausted Cincinnati fielders.

By the time the game-long bumbler ended, Doc had given up one homer, 20 singles, five doubles, and had allowed the Dodgers to score each inning. The game total was 26 hits and 21 runs!

Doc Parker set two records that day that have not been broken in 91 years. He established the National League record for most runs given up, and the record for most hits allowed in major league play!

94